Dedicated to Robin James and the memory of the real unicorn, Morgan. May they live forever in the Land of Later.

Stephen

Beyond the horizon in the middle of the Crystal Sea, is a beautiful island called Serendipity. On the northern slope of the island, where rolling hills turn to mountain splendor, was a small, wonderful kingdom called the Land of Later. In this kingdom there was a castle wherein lived a baker who was also the king, but that is yet another story.

This story is about the daughter of the baker, who was also the king, a young, beautiful princess, the Princess Robin Irene. No one called her by her formal name. They simply called her Princess.

She spent her days and nights dreaming of this, that and the other thing; whichever and whatever that and the other thing may be.

She did little else.

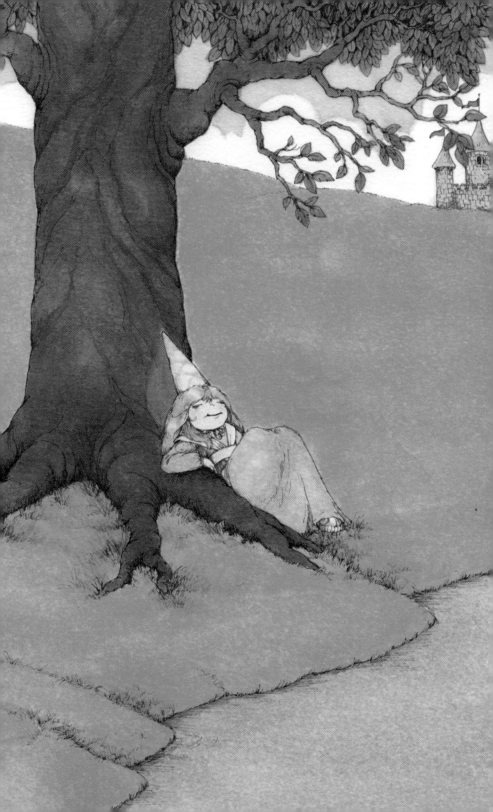

Life in the castle was governed by the king's simple rules. One of those rules was that when you woke in the morning you cleaned your room and made your bed.

Princess hated rules.

This morning, as on others, she woke, got dressed and went outside to play instead of cleaning her room. At the edge of the meadow that surrounded the castle she found a soft velvet-moss path that led deep into the forest. In all her play around the castle she had never seen this path before.

"I should go back and clean up my room," she said, knowing that she would get in trouble for not doing her chores. Then she laughed, "Oh, poof! Oh, piffle! I will clean up my room. I'll simply do it, just a little later."

With that she began skipping down the velvet-moss path.

Princess walked deeper and deeper into the forest. It was wonderful to find such a magical path so near the castle. The trees spread their boughs forming a beautiful canopy over her head and the velvet-moss path felt like plush carpet beneath her feet.

"I should start back before I get lost," she whispered to a bunny on the path.

Then she laughed and laughed. "Oh, poof! Oh, piffle! I will go back but just a little later!"

carily, the deeper she went into the forest, the darker it became. What had been bright and light, was now dark and very scary.

The gnarled old trees twisted their bark into ugly faces and their limbs, like scraggly arms, reached out for Princess who began running faster and faster.

"I should turn back!" she panted. "I should go home!"

"Oh, poof! Oh, piffle!" she puffed as she ran deeper and deeper into the forest.

"I'll go back. I will go back but just a little later!"

After what seemed like hours and hours of running she saw a glimmer of light streaming through the trees just ahead.

"That must be a meadow," she thought. "I will get out of the forest and catch my breath and then go back to the castle. . . just a little bit later."

With that she scurried and hurried down the velvet-moss path.

With a great sense of relief she stepped into the most beautiful of meadows. Flowers of every kind bloomed in clusters here and there.

"I should go home and do my chores," she said. "I should go home and eat my breakfast." She looked and thought and thought and looked.

"Oh, poof! Oh, piffle! I can do all of that later." And with that she set off to explore the magical meadow.

As she was looking about, she came upon a most peculiar sight; a unicorn with his twisted horn stuck in the branches of a tree. She moved closer and closer and finally politely asked, "Uh, excuse me, Mr. Unicorn, sir, but why are you standing with your horn stuck in the branches of the tree?"

"Oh, it is such a bother," said the unicorn, "my horn is caught in the tree. My name is Morgan and I have found myself here quite by accident."

Princess moved closer as Morgan told his tale.

This was Morgan's meadow and it was here that he lived and played. One of the games he loved to play best was tickle tag with the bumblebees that tended the honeycomb and the pollen harvest in the meadow.

He would toss his mane and gamely try to touch a buzzing bee flying by with his horn. It was a fun game and Morgan would run round and around chasing bumblebees on the wind trying to tickle them the best he could.

Yesterday, intent on catching the bees as they buzzed on their way, Morgan didn't look where he was going. One minute he was running free as could be and the next . . .

. . . he was tangled in the branches of the tree.

The bees felt bad and desperately tried to free Morgan's horn. But try though they may, the beautiful, twisted horn was stuck as stuck could be.

"And so you see, Princess, I have been trapped here for over a day. I am as hungry as can be, and my legs are tired from standing. Won't you please set me free?"

Princess thought for a moment or two. "Yes, Morgan, I truly will set you free, but just a little later. First I want to finish exploring the meadow. I will help you but just a little bit later."

With that she scampered off to look about the meadow leaving Morgan still tangled in the tree.

When Princess had seen all there was to see she finally wandered back to the poor unicorn.

"Oh, piffle! Oh, pooh!" she yawned. "I'm bored. I guess I can now help free you from the tree."

She looked about and found a sturdy stick. Then, she carefully climbed up the tree and sitting on the branch she prodded and pried, twisted and turned and soon Morgan was freed.

"Come on!" she shouted as she jumped from the tree. "Now you can play tag with me." With that she began running across the meadow looking over her shoulder as Morgan trotted behind.

As Morgan had already learned and Princess was about to learn, running without looking is not a good thing to do.

The Princess didn't see the lily-pond. She didn't stop. She didn't turn. She ran straight into the water.

With arms flopping and flailing she climbed upon a large green pad. Coughing and sputtering she called out, "Oh, poof! Oh, piffle! Help me Morgan. I can't swim!

"I'll help you Princess, but first I must get something to eat. I spent all night in the tree and I am just as hungry as can be."

"But, poof. But, piffle," sniffled Princess, "I want you to help me now, not later. I'm wet and cold and . . ."

And it was then that Princess realized what she had done to Morgan, and done all of her life: she had always put things off until later.

With a tear in her eye and lump in her throat Princess said, "I am so sorry, Morgan. I have lived my life in the Land of Later when I should have been living in the now. I promise you this, I won't ever put off to later what should be done now ever, ever again."

Morgan, touched by her words, leaned down and bowed to Princess. His great twisted horn reached across the water. Carefully Princess grabbed hold and he carefully lifted her from the pond.

Though she wanted to stay and play, Princess thanked Morgan for setting her free, then scampered back down the velvet-moss path. Later was now and she had chores to do in the castle.

This story is true
Though twisted of course
The Princess is an artist
And Morgan was a horse

More to this story at BookPop.com

When I first met Robin lebinty-billion years ago she shared with me her portfolio. One of the samples was a card she had made for her mother, the illustration being a Robin-esque little girl standing by a horse. She had delightfully captioned the card "Me by Golly!"

Golly was not the name of her real horse for he was a Morgan called Morgan. As the book took form in my imagination Robin was the Princess and Morgan played himself with a horn added for emphasis and fantasy. The story of procrastination came from me.